characters created by

# lauren child

# I'm really ever so NOT well

Grosset & Dunlap

# Charlie and Lola™

Text based on the script written by Samantha Hill

Illustrations from the TV animation produced by Tiger Aspect

GROSSET & DUNLAP
Published by the Penguin Group
Penguin Group (USA) Inc., 375 Hudson Street, New York, New York 10014, U.S.A.
Penguin Group (Canada), 90 Eglinton Avenue East, Suite 700, Toronto, Ontario, Canada M4P 2Y3
(a division of Pearson Penguin Canada Inc.)
Penguin Books Ltd, 80 Strand, London WC2R 0RL, England
Penguin Ireland, 25 St Stephen's Green, Dublin 2, Ireland
(a division of Penguin Books Ltd)
Penguin Group (Australia), 250 Camberwell Road, Camberwell, Victoria 3124, Australia
(a division of Pearson Australia Group Pty Ltd)
Penguin Books India Pvt Ltd, 11 Community Centre, Panchsheel Park, New Delhi - 110 017, India
Penguin Group (NZ), 67 Apollo Drive, Mairangi Bay, Auckland 1311, New Zealand
(a division of Pearson New Zealand Ltd.)
Penguin Books (South Africa) (Pty) Ltd, 24 Sturdee Avenue, Rosebank, Johannesburg 2196, South Africa

Penguin Books Ltd, Registered Offices:
80 Strand, London WC2R 0RL, England

Library of Congress Cataloging-in-Publication Data is available.

ISBN 978-0-448-44569-4          10 9 8 7 6 5 4 3 2 1

I have this little sister, Lola.
She is small and very funny.
Well, usually she's very funny,
but not when she's not feeling very well.
And today Lola's really not feeling well.

Lola has a cold.

I say, "How are you feeling, Lola?"

Lola says,
"I'm really, really
ever so not well,
     Charlie."

So I say,
"Mum's given me some pink
milk and cookies for you, Lola."

Pink milk is Lola's favorite.

But Lola says,

"**Yuck!**

My pink milk

tastes **green**.

And the cookies
are too **prickly**

to swallow.

I don't feel like
eating or drinking

**anything.**"

Then Lola says, "I remember when everything tasted yummy..."

So I say,
"Dad always says flowers are very good
at cheering little people up."

But Lola says,

"Aaaachoooooooooo!

chai

"They're not very good at
    cheering up this little person!"

Then Lola says,
"My **nose** hurts,
and nothing **smells**.

I remember when I used to be able to do **smelling**...

Then I have an **idea** how to **cheer** up Lola.

I say, "I know...
let's sing a **song**."

But Lola says,
"I can't do **singing**, Charlie...
my t**hroat** hurts and
my voice is all quiet."

Then she says, "I remember singing...

'The sun has got his hat on,

Hip, hip, hip Hooray,

The sun has got his hat on

And he's coming out today!'"

Lola says,
    "Can **you** sing for me, Charlie?"

    I say,
"I can't. I've got a big soccer game
        and I've promised Marv I'll play.
I **can't** break my promise."

"Pleeease, Charlie,"
says Lola.

So I say,
"All right then...

'If you're happy

and you know it

clap

your

hands...

Then I say,
    "You're not clapping, Lola."

"I'm not happy, Charlie," says Lola.
"Why do I feel so really, really not well?"

So I say, "It's those germs in your mouth."

"Germs?"
    says Lola.

And I say,
"Your cold germs. Would you
    like to see them, Lola?"

So I take Lola
to the bathroom
to look in the mirror.

Lola says,

"Ahhhhhhhhhhh..."

"There must be **thousands** and **hundreds** of germs, Charlie!

yippeee!

woohoooooooo!

1...2...3.....12...13...14...15....

54 billion....

a trillion..."

yeehaarr!

weyhaay!

Then I hear the phone ringing.
I say,
"It's probably Marv.
I'd better go and answer it."

Marv says,
"So, are you coming
to play soccer then?
It's a big game, you know!"

I say,
"Yes, it's just that Lola . . ."

"Charlieee! I feel really, really terribly **ever so NOT well**," says Lola.

And I say,
"I've just told Marv that
            I'm on my way. Mum says
she'll come and play with you."

And Lola says,
    "But I want **you**
to play with me, Charlie!"

So I say, "Okay.
How about a quick jigsaw puzzle?"

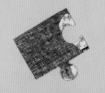

The smiley puzzle
is Lola's favorite.

Then I hear the phone
ringing again
and I know
it's going
to be Marv...

Marv says,
"So you're definitely
coming then?"

I say,
"Of course I am...
I'm coming...
right now!"

Lola says,
"Charlie! I want you
to stay...
Please?"

And then I have a really good idea.
"Hey, Lola," I say.
"Where's your butterfly gone...?"

"To Flutterby Mountain!" says Lola.

"Yes," I say.
"Do you want to try and catch him?"

Lola says,
"Do you think we can
catch Mr. Butterfly?"

"Quickly," I say,

"we're going to have to . . . cloud hop!"

Lola says, "I love cloud hopping, Charlie."

"Come here, fluttery butterfly,"
says Lola.
"Let me catch you..."

Then I hear
a knock at the door.

"Come on, Charlie!"
says Marv.

And I say,
"All ri...

Ah...

Ah...

Ah...

The next day, I'm in bed feeling really not well.
Lola says, "So, how are you feeling, Charlie?"

I say,
"I'm really . . . really
**not well, Lola!**"

And Lola says,
"Don't worry,
Charlie...

...because I'm going to be here every
minute of all day until you're
completely absolutely **better!**"

And I say,
"Muuummm!"